MIRRORS

written by The Wonder Twinzz

Illustrated and Designed by Fx color Studio

ACKNOWLEDMENTS

To God, my family and friends who have cheered The Wonder Twinzz on from the start, you know who you are LaConna, J.R., and Diamond we thank you for your continued support. To an amazing husband and awesome brother-in-law Chris Gittens thank you for all the support and dedication that you have poured into The Wonder Twinzz projects and ideas. Even if you had doubts about all the crazy things we came up with you never wavered and we are truly grateful. To Kameren Kim, thank you for the part you played in our first children's book. Thank you Crystal Pennymon for editing our book. Lastly, to all the children who reads this book and think that you are not good enough or not pretty enough. Just know that you are special and do not let anyone tell you any different- Just look in the mirror.

On a warm, sunny day Sonja skipped to the park to play softball.

She loved to play softball with her friends and hoped that one of her friends would be able to go and play with her.

After resting on the bench Sonja came to
a three-way stop at the end of the street.
There stood a mirror.

Sonja was very curious as to why a mirror was there,
so she walked up to the mirror.

In the mirror was a girl. "Hello." Sonja said to the girl, looking back at her in the mirror. "Hello." The girl spoke softly back. Sonja saw that the girl was very sad. " Are you okay?"

The girl held her head down, "I didn't think that you would want to talk to me." "Why?" Sonja asked, puzzled. In a softer voice the girl tried to answer Sonja." Because a grown-up did a bad touch to me. No one wants to be my friend, now."

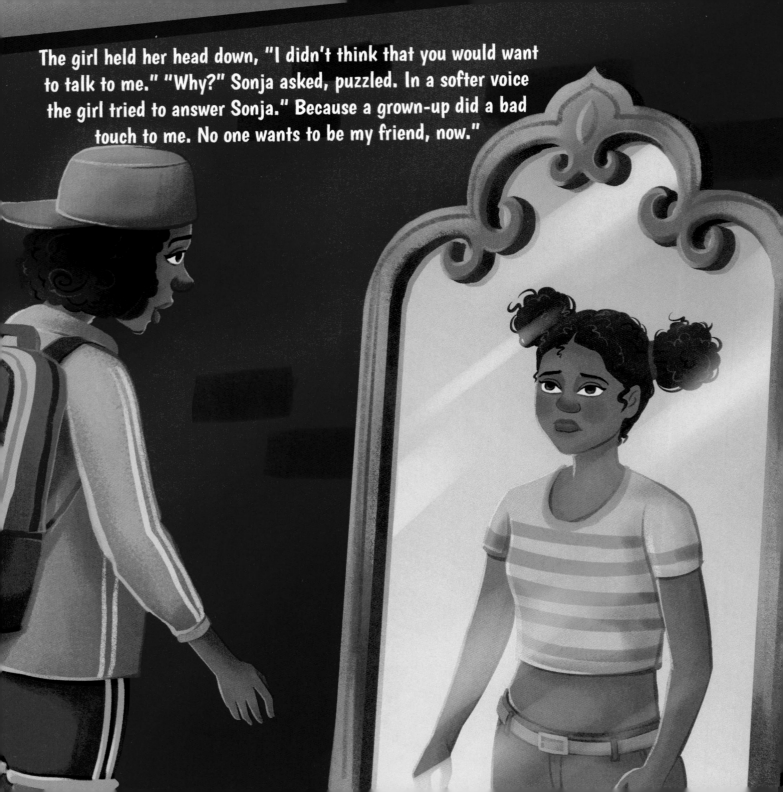

Sonja felt bad for the girl. She let her know that she would be her friend and invited her to go to the park.

Happily the girl jumped from the mirror to Sonja's backpack.

Sonja started her walk toward the park with the girl from the mirror on her back.

Sonja came to the end of a three-way street once again.

Sonja walked up to the mirror and
there inside of the mirror
stood yet another sad girl.

"Are you okay?" Sonya asked the sad girl.
"No. Look at me. I'm fat. No one
wants to be my friend."
The girl answered with more sadness.

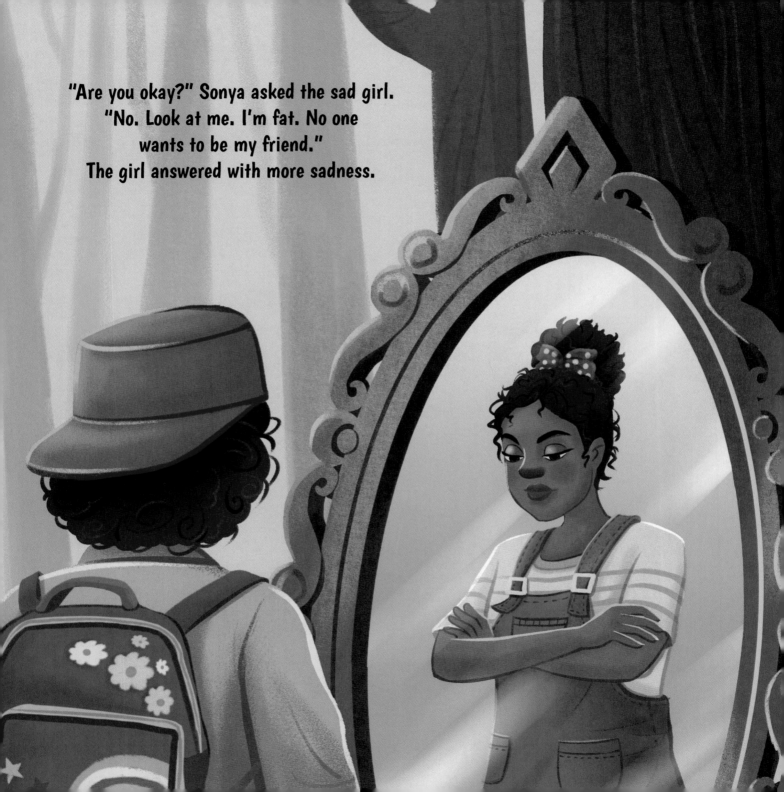

Sonja told the girl that she was pretty and that she was just fine.

She asked her if she would like to go with her and her friend to play softball at the park.

The girl in the mirror looked around, but answered, "I would love to go with you."

The second girl from the mirror jumped just as
happily into Sonja's backpack as the first one.
Sonja felt that everyone was full of joy as
she kept walking to the park.

Sonja finally made it to the park. The two girls from the mirror jumped out of the backpack. As the three of them came face-to-face with each other they saw that they all looked alike.

Sonja could feel what they were feeling, soon knowing that they were all the same person. As Sonja kept staring at herself she discovered that she was carrying herself the whole time. She knew that what she saw in the mirrors was herself.

She was the sad girl who had been treated badly by a grown-up and who was unhappy with herself because of her weight. She had been carrying the sadness on her back. All she wanted to do was to go to the park, play softball and be happy, but she stopped, looked in the mirrors and picked up bad feelings along the way.

She carried those bad feelings in her backpack. Sonja remembered that she was nice to both girls from the mirrors and that she would be their friend. So, she decided to not carry her bad feelings anymore, to be free and enjoy the park.

By treating herself good, she knew that she was worth more than what she had been through by......just looking in the mirror.